EMPRESS OF THE DARK

FORGOTTEN GODS #6

LAURA GREENWOOD

Contents

BLURB

For years, Nephthys has been living in the compound of a man that's never loved her. When a god from her past shows up, she's offered a chance to finally leave.

Despite being drawn to Heka and the life he offers her among the other gods, Nephthys finds herself refusing.

Until Seth pushes things too far and she realises she can't stand by and watch any longer.

But escaping is only half the challenge. Once she's back at Karnak, she has to persuade the other gods she can still be trusted.

-

Empress of the Dark is a fantasy/mythology romance and is part of the Forgotten Gods series and is Nephthys' complete story. It is based on Egyptian mythology.

A Note On The Gods & Goddesses Of The Forgotten Gods Universe

Due to the span of Ancient Egyptian history, many gods and goddesses took on multiple roles over the span of time (as demonstrated in <u>The Queen Of Gods Trilogy</u> by Hathor's multitude of aspects). The family links the Ancient Egyptians formed between their gods weren't meant to represent blood family, but aspect ties. This is why many of the gods and goddesses are consorts with their siblings. In the context of the Forgotten Gods Universe, none of the gods are related to one another by blood, but many choose to create family bonds.

You can see a full list of Gods & Goddesses in the Forgotten Gods Universe, as well as other definitions and information, <u>on my website</u>.

CHAPTER 1

I bit my lip, trying to stop myself from speaking out about the atrocities Seth was once again trying to commit. I was getting tired of sitting beside him while he did this. It hurt my heart, and not just because of the pain he was causing.

He hadn't always been like this. Early in our existence, he'd been sweet and kind. But seeing his brother's rise to true greatness had changed him. He'd no longer been the same person, and as the centuries passed, he'd become more bitter and twisted, and taken it out on the people around him.

I wasn't sure I'd be able to take it much longer.

"Your thoughts are showing, Your Eminence," one of the slaves said as she leaned in and poured me some wine.

I glanced at her face, readying myself to reprimand her for speaking out of turn, and insinuating that I was anything less than happy at my consort's show of aggression in front of us. I stopped myself, recognising her as the slave girl he'd whipped in front of everyone while Ra had been visiting. He'd killed her friend, too. I was reasonably sure her name was Rhodopis. I tried not to learn anyone's name in case it ended badly, but sometimes it couldn't be helped.

I nodded my thanks, not daring to speak it in case someone overheard us. There was no shortage of spies among those gathered here. And Seth wouldn't spare me because I was his wife. If anything, he'd be harder on me for it. I'd been there to see all of his many failures and he was never going to let either of us forget it.

The slave girl vanished, and I made a mental note to keep an eye on her to make sure she didn't get into more trouble. She'd probably be fine. She clearly understood how life in the compound worked, and that meant she'd be clever enough to avoid the potential pitfalls of living with Seth and his inability to control his temper.

"My Lady," a male voice said, pulling my attention away from my thoughts.

I turned to find Amun standing a few feet away, bowing deeply. I studied him intently, trying to work out what he was doing in Seth's compound, just like I did every other time I saw him. I didn't understand why he wasn't at Karnak with the other gods. It was where I'd be if I had the choice.

Sadly, I did not.

"Amun, it's a pleasure as always." I dipped my head. While I theoretically had more power within the compound, he had more outside it. Which was one of the reasons I was so confused about his presence here. Unlike with some of the lesser gods, Seth didn't have the ability to keep Amun here.

"I believe the pleasure is all mine, Nephthys. I've rarely seen such beauty as yours," he returned with the smooth charm he was renowned for.

I almost snorted. "Clearly you haven't seen Hathor in the past few centuries. I assure you, she far outshines me." Which was to be expected when considering she was the goddess of beauty. Among other things.

"Ah, but she is not here, and you are."

"Then I believe you're flattering for the sake of it," I retorted. "Pray tell me what your true purpose of striking up a conversation is?"

There was always something when it came to Amun. He'd been that way for as long as I could remember.

"What if I wanted your company?"

I laughed bitterly. "In which case, you don't value your life very much. You should know what Seth does to men who wanted that." I wasn't foolish enough to think that it was a good idea to be seen talking to him too much. Seth was quick to anger and prone to jealousy. Which was ridiculous when I knew he'd never loved me.

Amun's eyes turned dark, as if angered by the implication of Seth's violence. It was a fair reaction in some ways.

"While I wouldn't want to do anything to anger the emperor of this compound, I can assure you that he wouldn't harm me for spending time with you," Amun said.

He was probably right. Seth needed Amun too much. No one ever said it out loud, but there was a reason Seth's plans always failed. He needed the support of more powerful gods or he'd fail again.

"I heard a rumour that Mafdet was here," Amun said offhandedly as he took the seat beside me.

I raised an eyebrow, glad he'd finally said what he was here for. It was always a relief when people came out with it rather than dancing around the issue as if it didn't exist.

He grabbed an abandoned goblet of wine and took a swig. It probably didn't matter whose it was, they wouldn't argue with a god of Amun's stature drinking it.

"You want to know where she is?" That was what most people wanted when they asked for someone by name. And that was just in general. When it came to Mafdet, everyone wanted to know where she was. Not that I could tell anyone, even if I wanted to. The whereabouts of some of Seth's allies, and most of his prisoners, was a well-kept secret even I wasn't privy to.

"Not at all," Amun countered, swirling the wine in his goblet as he spoke. "I want to know how Seth convinced him. Mafdet's been stuck to Ma'at's side for thousands of years, and now she's broken away from her vendetta? It doesn't seem very likely to me."

"Are you suggesting she was blackmailed?" It wasn't outside the realms of possibility. But I had no idea how he'd lured the god of truth away.

"I'm not suggesting anything," Amun responded.

I only just refrained from rolling my eyes. Why did he have to be so difficult about this? I wasn't foolish enough to think he didn't know what he was doing.

"Then I have nothing to say about your accusation."

Amun chuckled, making me slightly uncomfortable. I hated that he was able to make me feel this way.

"You used to be one of the most formidable goddesses in the world, Nephthys. What happened to you?"

Anger flared up inside me, and my wings longed to burst free in a show of power I hadn't expressed in a long time. I squashed my feelings down. I didn't want him to know that he'd gotten to me.

Nor did I want anyone else to know the true extent of what I could still do. "I grew up and realised there was more to life than intimidating people," I said coolly. "I'd suggest you try it."

Amun raised an eyebrow. "And there she is." While the way he said the words suggested I'd done exactly what he'd expected me to, it also seemed as if he was pleased that I had. I couldn't even begin to fathom why.

"And here I go," I responded tartly as I rose to my feet, refusing to pay him any more attention than I already had.

I gestured for my serving girls to follow me. I could have left them behind, but that would put them at Seth's mercy, and I wasn't willing to do that. There wasn't much I could do to help anyone, but I could do this.

Amun laughed to himself, the sound following me even as I strode away from the banqueting table.

I resisted the urge to turn and glare at him, knowing that it would only raise more questions among those assembled.

I moved quickly, eager to get back to my rooms so I could avoid a run-in with the last person in Egypt that I wanted to see.

"Nephthys," Seth growled.

Too late.

I closed my eyes and took a deep breath as I tried to steady my nerves.

Slowly, I turned to face him. "My Lord Consort," I responded smoothly, hating every word. Most of the gods in marriages as unhappy as ours had gone their separate ways centuries ago, and yet he wouldn't allow me to. "How can I help you?"

"Why are you leaving?" he demanded.

I gestured for the surrounding servants and slaves to leave us. I didn't want them to be in Seth's way when he was as annoyed as he currently seemed to be. Not that it was all that possible to tell if he was angrier than normal. He always seemed annoyed at the world.

"The sun was getting too much for me," I lied.

Seth's expression darkened. It was a blatant lie. I'd lived in Egypt my entire life, the desert sun wasn't something that bothered me. Though I was a little surprised he knew that. He hadn't paid attention to me in years.

"What did Amun want?"

"To cause trouble." I suspected that was true.

Seth let out a dissatisfied noise that probably came about because he could *do* anything to the other god. Amun could cause as many problems as he wanted to, Seth was never going to be able to retaliate.

It was almost amusing.

When Seth didn't say anything else, I took my chance and dipped my head before disappearing towards my rooms. There was a small chance he'd call me back, but I didn't think he would.

He'd be too busy trying to work out precisely what Amun was up to and not give another thought to me until tomorrow at the earliest.

CHAPTER 2

T he warm water of the bath seeped into my skin and took away some of the tension of the day. Though not all of it.

Nothing could do that. Living in this compound could never be called relaxing, even if I was supposed to be the second most important person in it. I guessed it had been too long since I'd believed that for me to feel I really was.

At least being a supposed Empress had the perks of me being able to bathe in peace. I imagined many of the other goddesses in the compound didn't have the luxury.

Frustration grew within me at the reminder that Seth had decided to start referring to himself as an Emperor. I had no idea what was going through his head when he'd chosen to do that, or how he thought he could be the Emperor of a single compound. He had no control over anything outside these walls, no matter how much he wanted to pretend he did. And the worst part was that we were all expected to go along with it regardless of if we knew the truth or not.

I closed my eyes and dipped my head back so I could wash my long dark hair. I ran my hands through it, untangling the knots through the water. It was a relief that I no longer had to wear a wig, even for special occasions. Time had moved on without us, and my status as a goddess wasn't recognised in most parts of the world.

If I was realistic, it was barely recognised in this compound.

Not for the first time, I found myself wishing I was at Karnak. And not just because I'd be able to do my job there. The calls to the Hall of Judgement were far fewer than they used to be, but each time I heard the call, it was painful not to heed it. But Seth didn't want me going. He either feared that the other gods would take me captive in an effort to weaken him, or he feared that I would choose to leave him and stay there. The latter option was one I'd found myself dreaming of more than once. The former wasn't the worst outcome either. Anything that got me out of Seth's control was good as far as I was concerned.

The water sloshed loudly against the sides of the bathing pool as I pulled my head from underneath it. I reached for my hair oil, only to freeze as footsteps sounded from the entrance to the baths. Fear settled in my stomach despite the fact I wasn't doing anything wrong.

"I'm sorry to interrupt your bath, Your Eminence," the slave girl from earlier said as she entered the room. "You had an urgent message that needed delivering."

I frowned. "Who is it from?" No one ever sent me letters. Or if they did, they always got stopped before I got them.

"I'm not sure, Your Eminence…"

"You don't have to keep calling me that when we're alone." I hated the honorific at the best of times, but when I was naked in the bath, it felt extra wrong.

She nodded. "I was just asked to deliver it to you and then to make sure it's destroyed once you've read it."

"Who told you that?" Despite my reservations, I reached out to take the letter from her, not worrying about my wet hands. If she was going to make sure the letter was destroyed anyway, then I didn't need to worry about it.

"One of the other slaves. I didn't recognise him."

This was getting stranger and stranger.

I unfolded the square of papyrus and scanned the message within. There was something familiar about the brushstrokes within, but it had been too long since I'd received a letter for me to be sure about who had written it.

"Do you know what's inside this?" I asked.

She shook her head. "I didn't read it."

So she could read? That was surprising. I suspected she must have learned before she came to the compound, or the slaves had been teaching one another. Seth would never have allowed them to learn for fear that they'd reveal his secrets to his enemies.

It made sense, but it was just another thing that added to my hatred of him, especially when it had been thousands of years since owning slaves had been made illegal amongst the gods. Yet he insisted on ignoring the rules. I wished I was able to do more to stop him. Instead, I was limited to making sure I treated everyone well regardless of their station within the compound, and helping in the small ways I could.

"The sender wants me to destroy this?" I asked, waving the papyrus to make it clear what I was talking about."

She nodded. "That was what I was told when I was given the letter to give to you."

"Okay, thank you."

She opened her mouth, almost as if she wanted to say something, but thought better of it.

I considered showing her a gesture of trust and suggesting that she should be the one that destroyed it for me, but I thought better of it. I had no idea who the sender of the message was, but they wanted me to meet them in the oasis outside of Seth's compound. That was dangerous, and I didn't want the information getting into the wrong hands, even if I didn't end up doing as the letter-writer wanted me to.

Slowly, I lowered the papyrus into the water and watched as the ink started to smudge and run, and then for it to drift into pieces, destroyed and illegible.

"Will there be a return message?"

I shook my head. "No, thank you. I wouldn't know who to send it to if there was." A small part of me wondered whether it was Seth testing my loyalty. That wasn't the kind of thing I'd put past him. But I knew his brushstrokes and these weren't them. I supposed he could have gotten someone else to write the words for him, but he wouldn't have thought about that. The only manageable thing about Seth's cruelty was that he liked to exercise it himself. He'd never let anyone do this for him.

She bowed her head in response. "Can I get anything else for you?"

"No thank you, Rhodopis."

She did a double-take probably not expecting me to have remembered her name. I smiled reassuringly at her so she knew I wasn't about to use it against her.

Rhodopis bowed low and left the baths, leaving me alone to contemplate the contents of my letter. I wasn't sure what I'd expected, but it wasn't a request from an unknown person to meet me in the oasis outside of Seth's compound.

While I knew the one the letter referred to, I didn't think I'd ever been there before, which didn't mean anything.

The real mystery was who had sent the letter in the first place. The cynical part of me thought it might have come from Seth himself in an attempt to trap me into leaving the compound. I wasn't sure what that would achieve, especially as he'd never explicitly told me that I couldn't.

But who else could it possibly be?

If I was feeling brave, I might be able to find out.

CHAPTER 3

I was a fool. That was the only explanation for me trying to sneak out of the compound. I supposed I could have used the main entrance, but without knowing what waited for me in the oasis, that didn't seem like the best idea.

But my curiosity had gotten the better of me.

I pulled my head scarf lower over my face in an attempt to obscure my features. I wasn't sure it would work very well if anyone knew me, but I was counting on the fact they didn't. Even so, it was a gamble. And if I was caught, it wasn't going to be easy to explain what I was doing in a way that would actually get me out of trouble.

I checked both ways, wanting to make sure there was no one coming. Once I was, I hurried down the path between buildings, trying to listen for any signs of other people over the pounding of my heart and the slap of my sandals against the ground.

I paused at the next crossroads and glanced over my shoulder, almost completely missing the guards heading my way from the opposite direction.

I froze, unable to process what was happening and what the best thing to do was.

A hand closed around my wrist and it was all I could do not to let out a small cry of alarm.

"It's only me," Rhodopis whispered and tugged me into a small gap between a couple of huts. There was barely enough room to breathe.

Before I was able to say anything to her about it, the guards strode past, their low murmurs almost close enough that I could tell what they were saying.

"Thank you," I whispered.

She nodded curtly. "You want to leave the compound, right?"

I opened my mouth to form some kind of denial, but it didn't come. "How did you know?"

"You covered it well, but I could see how shocked you were when you read the letter, it had to be something like that."

"Oh."

"I can help you, if you'll let me," she offered.

"Why would you do that? Seth won't be able to do much to me, but we both know that isn't true for you. He could kill you."

"He can't, actually," she responded. "I'm not a demi-goddess."

My eyes widened as the implications of what she was saying sunk in. I hadn't paid much attention to the compound in the past few thousand years, but I knew she'd been with us for that long. The only way that was possible was if she was a demi-goddess. Or a full one.

"How has that gone unnoticed?" I asked. Seth would have elevated her from her position as a slave here if he did, though I wasn't sure that was necessarily a good thing.

"I didn't know myself until fairly recently," she admitted. "But that's beside the point. I keep quiet about it because it's safer."

"That's wise," I agreed.

"And now you know one of my secrets in exchange for one of yours," Rhodopis said. "So would you like me to help you get out of the compound?"

I nodded. "But I'll need to get back in."

She smiled knowingly, though I wasn't sure why. I had no idea who I was going to meet, or what was going to happen in the oasis. She couldn't have one for me.

"I'll be able to wait around the gate until dawn. Whistle twice when you arrive back at it. If I respond, then it'll be safe to come back in, if I don't, then you'll have to wait or find another way back in."

"Thank you."

"You're welcome. We need to go this way." She pulled me through the small gap and out the other side.

The walkway between these huts was smaller than the one on the other side, and wasn't lit nearly as well. If I'd thought things through, perhaps I'd have come down this one in the first place. But there was no point dwelling on what might have been when there was nothing that could be done about it now.

I followed Rhodopis through the twists and turns of the compound, seeing it in a completely different light to the way I normally did. Or more accurately, seeing it in the lack of light. While I wasn't going to pretend I was Seth's right-hand woman or anything even approaching that, it was clear that the experience I had living here was one that didn't match what the rest of the population did.

Not for the first time, I found myself wishing for change while feeling powerless to make it happen. Perhaps if I was back at Karnak I'd be able to. But the longer I spent here, the less likely it was that the others would take me back.

After about ten minutes, we came to the wall that encircled the entire compound, and a small door carved into the side of it.

"I didn't know this was here," I said.

Rhodopis smiled wryly. "Not many people do. But if you didn't know about the door, how were you going to get out?"

"I was going to fly," I admitted. "It wasn't the best plan. The door is a lot better."

"People might notice a woman flying through the air," Rhodopis said.

"I'd have turned into a kite," I assured her. "No one would have thought anything of it." Probably. It might still be a good idea to try that, but it had been so long since I'd changed forms that I didn't want to risk having forgotten how to fly in a crucial moment. Not that I was going to admit that to anyone. I wanted them to think I was still at the height of my power, even if it wasn't true.

"Oh, I thought you just had wings in this form."

"I have those too," I assured her. "But they're a bit more noticeable."

"I can't say I disagree. Anyway, if you go through here and head straight on, you'll come to the oasis in about half an hour. I doubt anyone will be out there."

"Thank you."

She simply nodded in response. "I'll be waiting for you to return here. I'll have to head to my chores at dawn." The implication that I was on my own if I was out that long hung in the air between us. She didn't need to warn me. I would be back well before then.

Rhodopis ushered me through the door and shut it behind me, not even waiting to make sure I got through okay.

But it didn't matter. Now I was on my way and would be at the oasis soon. I didn't know whether I was more nervous or excited to find out what was waiting for me there.

Chapter 4

The oasis was lush and fresh in a way the desert surrounding Seth's compound definitely wasn't. All around me, the sounds of life and nature filled the air, welcoming me to the tranquil spot in the middle of nowhere.

I couldn't believe I'd never been here before. Or that Seth hadn't destroyed it yet. Maybe there was something magical about the oasis that meant he couldn't.

A small path wound its way through the trees, and I followed it despite not knowing whether I was heading in the right direction or not. This seemed like the most logical path, but my letter hadn't specified where I was supposed to go other than the oasis as a whole.

The further in I got, the less I worried about this being a trap from Seth. He might enjoy toying with people, but I doubted he had the patience to wait this long into my journey before revealing the truth about it.

The path ended, opening up into a small clearing surrounding a glistening lake. I scanned the scene in front of me, even more amazed than I had been before.

My gaze landed on a familiar form striding into the clearing, causing my heart to skip a beat.

"Heka?" There was no keeping the surprise out of my voice. The god of healing and magic was the last person I'd expected to find waiting for me in the oasis. Thousands of years ago, just after Seth had first shown his true colours, I'd thought that there could be something between Heka and me But it was a foolish dream born out of misery.

"Good evening, Nephthys," he responded with a dip of his head. "You haven't changed."

I arched an eyebrow. "It's been several thousand years."

"And yet your beauty has grown stronger than ever."

"How could I have done that if I haven't changed?" I asked, though I was mostly trying to cover up how much his words meant to me. Unlike the flattery that came from Amun and the other gods like him, I could tell that Heka meant it.

"Magic," he responded with a surprisingly cheeky grin. "And before you argue that isn't possible, you should remember that I'm an expert on the subject."

I resisted the urge to roll my eyes. "Then I feel it's my duty to remind you that you once told me that magic was an inscrutable force and the mysteries of it would never be unravelled, even by you."

"I could say that I was an idealistic god with barely a few centuries of experience."

"As opposed to what you are now?" I asked.

"You mean an idealistic god with barely a few millenniums of experience."

My soft snort of amusement took me off guard. How long had it been since I'd made a noise like that? It was best if I didn't think about it.

"I think you can claim the title of experienced by this point," I assured him.

"I shall add Nephthys approved to my list of achievements."

I shook my head in bemusement, shocked at how easy it was to be around him. Maybe it was because I was away from the compound and not having to deal with the fear of Seth's wrath coming down on me for no apparent reason.

"Would you like to sit?" Heka asked, gesturing towards the side of the lake that dominated the oasis.

I considered for a moment. It looked like a beautiful place to rest, but could I risk staying here any longer than I already had? I had no idea whether or not Seth would come looking for me this evening, but it was almost certain that *someone* would, and if they found me missing, I had no idea what would happen.

"It isn't a trap," he assured me. "Just a conversation."

"Sometimes they can be the same thing," I muttered.

"Not with me. I'm not..."

He didn't finish his statement, presumably thinking better of insulting the man who was technically still my husband. Our marriage would only end if I moved out of his compound. Sometimes, that seemed like an easy thing to achieve, but that never lasted. A small part of me knew that no matter where I went, Seth would be able to find me, and I didn't want to think about what he'd do when he did.

"I'll sit," I said eventually. "But I won't stay long."

Heka nodded, seeming to understand my predicament. He'd always been a perceptive person. It put some of the other gods and goddesses off, but it had never done that to me. I liked someone who was able to see the world for what it was and make the most of it.

The ground was still warm from the heat of the day's sun, but the breeze coming off the water added a pleasant refreshing note that I wasn't used to.

"It's beautiful here," I said.

"It is," Heka agreed. "Do you come here often?"

I grimaced. "I've never been here before today." I had no idea how I'd managed to miss so much beauty right outside the compound. I often felt confined within the walls, but never as much as I did in this moment. It drove home how little freedom I had, and how long the problem had been going on for.

Now I just had to work out how to change that.

"Why did you ask me to come?" I'd been distracted by the identity of my companion and had forgotten what I needed to know.

Heka sighed. "You're not going to like it."

"I'll like it even less if you don't tell me," I pointed out.

"You never were one for games."

I chuckled dryly. "I don't see the point in saying things you don't mean just to play with the other person."

"But you see the point in saying them at other times?"

I shrugged. "Sometimes you have to tell a lie in order to survive. That's not saying something you don't mean for a game, that's saying what you don't mean in order to see another day."

Sadness flashed over his face. It disappeared quickly, but not fast enough for me to have missed it.

"Things haven't gotten better between you and Seth?"

Surprise flitted through me. I didn't think he'd actually come out and ask me that. "Did you think they would?"

"No. It's why I'm here."

I cocked my head to the side, confused by what he was on about. I smoothed my hand over the short grass beside me, mostly for something to occupy myself with while waiting for him to elaborate.

Heka sighed. "This is harder than I thought it would be."

"To talk about how much my husband is a bad person?" I asked. "Surely you wouldn't have thought it was going to be easy."

"It's not that. But it's also not-not that."

"You're starting to play games with your words," I warned him, though I wasn't sure why. I was too intrigued by what he was trying to achieve to get up and walk away, especially when he seemed close to telling me what this was all about.

"Some of the others have wondered about whether or not you're happy here."

"They don't wonder enough to send me any letters," I murmured.

"Isis writes to you every week," he said.

I blinked a few times. It was one thing to think that I wasn't getting the messages I was supposed to, it was another to have confirmation of it. I thought Isis had turned her back on me after she heard the rumours about me having her husband's baby. There was nothing in the rumour. I had no idea where Anubis had come from or who his parents were, but it certainly wasn't from me and Osiris.

But it turned out my fears had been unfounded. Isis might be my sister in name only, but she still wanted me in her life. That meant the world to me, even if I hadn't been getting her letters.

"Please tell her I'm sorry. I've written to her over the years too, but I've never gotten any of her letters."

"She assumed you hadn't," Heka assured me. "Or at least, she does now. She did go through a period of anger towards you in the thirteen-hundreds."

"That's to be expected." I'd gone through one of my own aimed at her at some point too.

Heka reached out as if he was going to touch my hand and offer me some comfort, but thought better of it. Instead, he took a deep breath. "I was sent here to ask you to return to Karnak with me."

My eyes widened. "Why you?"

"In truth, I volunteered."

"Why?"

"You're full of questions."

"And you're full of mysteries," I pointed out. "What am I supposed to do? Blindly follow what you say just because you're the one to say it?"

He chuckled. "No."

"Then you'll tell me why you volunteered for this." I was more than a little intrigued about why he'd decided to do this. He was risking a lot by being so close to Seth's compound, especially his freedom. Heka might not be the most remembered god out there, but he was still a powerful one, and

I dreaded to think what would happen if he was caught.

"I'm not sure," he admitted. "I just had this feeling that it should be me who came to see you. Don't you ever have moments like that?"

"I came here," I pointed out. "I wasn't sure whether or not I would until the last minute. How did you even get a message to me if you thought I was unreachable?"

"I can't tell you that, I'm sorry."

"Ah, you have a spy inside the compound. I thought as much."

"What gave it away?"

"I've been around for a very long time. I suspect several of the gods and goddesses have someone on the inside. Ma'at certainly does. I imagine Ra does as well." And that was only scratching the surface. I wouldn't be surprised if half of the demi-gods within Seth's compound were spies for one person or another.

"Which means Seth has spies at Karnak."

"Of course he does. Though from the way he talks about them, I'm not sure they're very good."

They were probably treated too well there and didn't want that to change.

Heka chuckled. "I can't say I feel bad about that."

"I don't expect you to."

We lapsed into silence as each of us thought over our conversation.

"I can't come with you," I said after a while. "As much as I would love to return to Karnak, I can't risk a war to do it. I might not be missed for a few hours, but anything more than that and I will be. I can't risk doing that to the world, I hope you can understand that."

"I do. I don't like it. You deserve your freedom too. But I understand why you feel that way."

I smile sadly at him. "Please believe me when I say that I wish things could be different." Going back to Karnak would be a dream come true. But it was going to have to stay just that.

A dream. One I'd never be able to achieve.

From the expression on Heka's face, he felt similarly about it. He wished it could be different, but knew that I was right.

"I should be getting back." I got to my feet before he could offer me an argument that would make me stay and consider his offer again. It wouldn't take much for me to cave. I never claimed that I wasn't selfish. "But I really appreciate you coming. Please tell Isis that I love her and miss her."

"Of course I will, but I think she already knows."

I smiled sadly. "I'm sure she does." No one ever accused Isis of not being empathic.

I didn't waste any more time and turned to head through the trees and back towards the starkly barren compound with a weight in my heart that hadn't been there before.

While I was touched that the other gods had been thinking about me and my well being, all it had done was remind me of everything I didn't have.

CHAPTER 5

S ilence reigned over the room as we all waited for Seth to arrive and say whatever it was he called us here to say. He didn't often have council sessions like this, or if he did, he didn't invite me. Despite the fact he wasn't even in the room yet, nobody talked. Even Amun was uncharacteristically silent. Perhaps everyone sensed that there was something bad coming our way. I hoped it wasn't my fault. If Seth had caught wind of the fact the gods at Karnak were actively trying to get people back to their side of whatever Seth was planning. It always went like this. The gods picked sides, sometimes different ones from the last time Seth tried something, and then there was an attempt from him to gain power that invariably failed.

I wasn't sure why he still tried. My only theory was that his purpose of creating storms and maintaining the balance of chaos in the world had tainted him and made him go out of the way to cause more of it. I secretly hoped that someone would be able to teach him how to control it and not make him lose himself over it. He really could be sweet and loyal when he tried. That man had just disappeared over the years and become someone I didn't recognise.

I scanned the faces of the other gods and goddesses in the room, taking note of who was here and what they might be thinking. Unsurprisingly, Anat wasn't her usual over flirty self. I'd come to realise a long time ago that she was faking it in order to get people to leave her alone. It was a trick that seemed to work. Most people dismissed her as a minor concubine of Seth's, but I couldn't forget the moment she'd joined the Egyptian pantheon. She and her sister had been covered in blood from a battle they'd been destined to lose from the beginning. It wasn't for lack of trying. Anat could be ruthless and deadly. At some point, she was going to reveal that side of herself again, and the people who had underestimated her would pay the price.

None of the other gods or goddesses in the room surprised me. I wasn't sure which of them were here because they wanted to be, or which truly believed in Seth's cause. I suspected the answer was very few of them. As far as I knew, several had been blackmailed to Seth's side, though I wasn't aware of which gods they were.

As with all of the other meetings I'd attended, Mafdet was conspicuously missing. Amun must be disappointed, though I was starting to question whether or not Seth actually had the goddess here at all. It wouldn't surprise me if it turned out it was all a ruse to put Ma'at ill at ease.

I had no idea what the truth was, and I doubted I'd ever find out. Some things weren't worth asking about or drawing attention to.

One of Seth's attendants scampered into the room with a panicked expression on his face. Either Seth was in a very bad mood, or his attendant had done something wrong and he was worried about being punished for it. I hoped for his sake that it was the former.

Seth strode into the room with a scowl on his face and an expression that could stop someone cold in their tracks.

This wasn't going to be a very pleasant meeting.

"We have a traitor in our midst," he growled, making everyone sit a little bit straighter.

Carefully, I made note of how each of them reacted, hoping it would reveal something useful to me. None of them were giving anything away, but at least I'd be able to use the information I gathered here in order to make a different assessment if something else happened.

"Karnak seems to be gaining information on our operations that is meant to be kept secret," he said. "There's only one way they can be doing that."

I almost rolled my eyes. His insistence that the modern world didn't exist was going to prove to be his downfall at some point. With Ma'at and Maahes in charge of the gods at the main temple, there was no doubt in my mind that they'd be using everything available to them in order to get information, including using modern technology that humans had developed over the past few hundred years. Combined with the magic they had access to, and the rich resources of the temple, and there was a good chance they knew the exact words we were saying at the moment we said them.

A small part of me hoped that was true and that it would mean they'd finally be able to contain Seth until he got the help he needed. I didn't want to be part of his rehabilitation, in fact, I'd rather never see him again, but that didn't mean I wanted the worst for him.

"How can we find out who it is, My Lord?" Khnum asked.

"I have my ways," Seth responded firmly, pacing up and down and staring at each of the gods in turn.

Anat sat up even straighter, before remembering who she was facing and replacing her serious expression with an inviting smile. I had to admit that she was good. Far better than I'd ever been at the art of seduction.

Seth passed her over without even pausing. He turned to Amun, narrowing his eyes. I was sure a part of him would love to accuse Amun of crossing him, but he didn't dare.

"Seth, I don't think anyone here is going to have turned on you," I said, not knowing where the words came from.

He swivelled to face me, anger leeching off every part of him as he glared at me for daring to speak. "What would you know?" he demanded.

I took a deep breath. This wasn't going the way I'd intended it to, and now things could get dangerous for me. "I spend my time in the compound talking to the other gods. I don't think any of them would be reporting back to Karnak on you."

Amun raised an eyebrow at me, probably surprised that I was vouching for anyone. Perhaps I should have spent the past few thousand years making allies of my own instead of assuming that no one was going to want to because of who my husband was. Thankfully, Seth had his back to the god and was oblivious of his facial expression.

"Get out," Seth demanded, pointing at the door. "You know nothing about any of this. I don't know why you're here."

I bit my tongue, knowing it wasn't helpful if I argued against him. He wouldn't believe a word I said, regardless of if it was true or not.

I rose to my feet and dipped my head in acknowledgement of his supposed superiority. It was mostly for show. I knew the consequences of not doing things Seth's way, and sometimes it was easier to just do it his way after all.

With my head held high, I made my way outside, glad to be free of his ridiculous council meeting where he accused his closest allies of spying on him. Everyone knew that wasn't the way to keep people on his side, but he insisted on doing it anyway.

I turned the corner to head back to my rooms only to end up frozen in my tracks at the sight of Heka talking to a slave. I blinked a few times, wondering whether it was my mind playing tricks on me because I wanted to see him and to believe what he'd said about the gods wanting me back at Karnak.

He didn't disappear.

At least he was dressed in slave clothing, though that could also be dangerous if the wrong person realised he was here.

The woman he was talking to turned slightly and I caught sight of a familiar profile. Rhodopis.

Everything clicked into place. She'd delivered his message to me because she was his contact within the compound. And if she was his, then that meant she was probably everyone else's too.

Seth was right. There was a spy in the compound, but he was looking in completely the wrong place.

CHAPTER 6

I unclipped my jewelled collar and set it down on my dressing table, followed by the golden rings from my hair, and the bracelets from around my wrists. I loved the intricacy of the designs and the way they looked on me, but I didn't need to wear them when I was alone.

Footsteps sounded outside the room, but I ignored them. It would probably just be one of my attendants bringing me clothes from the laundry building. It wasn't anything they needed my help or assistance with.

"Nephthys."

I spun around at the sound of Heka's voice to find him standing in the door to my bedchamber. He was still dressed in his slave clothes, though this close, he wasn't very convincing. They were too new and not worn in nearly as much as they should be.

"Heka."

"You don't seem surprised to see me."

"I'm not," I admitted. "I saw you."

"Ah, I thought you might have. May I come in?" he asked.

I should say no, but a large part of me didn't want to. I enjoyed his company, and it had been a long since someone had cared about spending time with me. I found myself nodding before I'd thought enough about it.

There was no going back now.

He stepped inside and closed the door.

"Bolt it," I instructed him.

"Won't someone question that?" Even as he questioned me, he slid it into place.

If anyone comes looking for me, you'll hide and I'll say I was trying to sleep. But no one's going to come. I've just been thrown out of one of Seth's council sessions, they'll be worried that my misfortune will rub off on them."

"That's not very fair."

"I don't blame them." I gestured towards the small table with two chairs in the corner of the room. A Hounds and Jackals board was set up in the middle, unplayed for centuries. It had been my favourite game in my youth, but I didn't have anyone to play in recent years.

Without me even suggesting it, Heka started to set up the board for us to play.

I took a seat, not stopping him even though I knew I should. He was already in my room, and that wasn't good. Neither was the fact he was in the compound at all.

"What are you doing here?" I asked. "If you get caught..."

"I'm not going to," he said. "I doubt any of the gods here would recognise me, and even if they did, they'll just think that I'd converted to this side."

"And if that happens and they ask Seth about it?" I didn't like the idea of what would happen to him if he was caught.

"Then I suppose I'll have to make sure that doesn't happen. Do you want to be the hounds or the jackals?"

"Hounds. But don't think you can distract me with the game. What you're doing is dangerous. Seth has no qualms in keeping people prisoner. No one knows where Mafdet is, I have to think she's being kept prisoner here."

"Mafdet defected of her own free will," Heka said. "I'm not sure where she is, but I can assure you she's there willingly. Do you know where Seth is keeping Wadjet?"

My eyebrows shot up. "He has Wadjet?" I hadn't even realised the protector goddess had been caught. This was bad news for Ma'at and the rest of the gods at Karnak.

"We think so, but no one knows for sure."

"I'm sorry I can't help. But I can see if I can find anything out."

"Don't. It's too dangerous."

"Just like it is for you to be here trying to get information out of me. What if I turned you into Seth?"

"You wouldn't."

"And what makes you so sure of that?" I picked up the knucklebones and threw them, unable to resist the pull of playing the game, even if I knew it was foolish.

A four. That was no good, I needed a five to move my piece onto the board.

"I know you, Nephthys."

"You knew me," I corrected. "A long time ago. A lot has changed since then."

"Has it?" He picked up the bones and threw them, only rolling a two. "From where I'm sitting, it looks like thousands of years have passed."

"The humans have moved on from us, they no longer believe like they once did." I threw the bones. A three. Also no good if I wanted to get on the board.

"They might not believe in us anymore, but that hasn't really changed anything. We go about our lives with less magic than before, but has that really made a difference? We eat, we drink, we fall in love, we..."

"Plot to take over the world," I finished dryly.

"Only if we're Seth."

"Is what Ma'at's doing really any better? Seth has his faults, and many of them. I can't deny that and nor will I. But the world needs chaos in order to have balance. It seems a little short-sighted of Ma'at to want to cut that out."

Heka sighed. "I can see your point, but maybe that's exactly it. Ma'at and Seth are at war with one another because that's what they're supposed to do." His bones finally rolled a five and he moved his first jackal onto the board.

"Then they should stop dragging the rest of us into their battle."

"You probably aren't wrong."

"I'm not." My throw was finally a five and I moved my hound onto the board.

I picked up the knuckles and handed them to Heka, our fingers brushing against one another as he took them from me, sending tingles up my arm.

I coughed and pulled away, unsure what to make of my reaction to him.

"You still haven't told me why you're here," I pointed out. "And I don't think it's to find out where Seth's prisoners are. You clearly have better placed spies to help with that."

"Ah, you noticed that."

"Or just have enough common sense to realise it's the case. If I was Ma'at, I'd have spies in as many places as possible, even those that didn't seem like they'd need one."

"You should be careful, Nephthys, or I'm going to start thinking you're one of Ma'at's spies," he teased.

I let out a small snort of amusement. "I'd be a terrible spy, and everyone knows it. Seth doesn't trust me."

"That's not true."

I raised an eyebrow. "He just threw me out of his meeting because he didn't believe I had anything important to say."

"What was the meeting even about?"

"The fact that he thinks there's a spy in the compound. You should be careful, if he finds out you're here, he'll assume it's you."

"I doubt he'll even notice if I stay wearing slave clothing."

I moved my piece forward a few spaces on the board. "Maybe. But don't gamble with your safety. And tell anyone that you know is spying to be extra careful too. I don't want to see anyone getting hurt over this." Or worse. Any demi-god spies could end up losing their lives if Seth discovered they'd been feeding information back to Ma'at. I didn't want to see that happen if a small comment to Heka could save them.

He gave me a strange look, almost as if he was pleased but not surprised by my statement. "I'll make sure that everyone is safe."

"Thank you." Perhaps it wouldn't help. Or it would help the wrong people. Seth was already convinced that there was a spy in the compound, he could easily turn his anger and frustration towards someone innocent. That was the risk we all took in living here.

"Have you given any more thought to my request?" Heka asked as he moved one of his jackals into the home space on his side of the board. If he got four more into it, then I'd lose.

"I gave you my answer already."

He sighed. "I know, but I'd hoped you'd change your mind."

"I can't."

"But you said yourself that we were heading towards a war between Seth and Ma'at anyway. Leaving the compound isn't going to change that, even if you want it to."

There was more truth in his words than I wanted to admit. But there was still a part of me that was reeling against going and potentially making things worse.

"I can't. Not yet."

Relief flashed over his face. "So it's only a partial no?"

I let out a loud sigh. "I suppose so. I want to come to Karnak, it's something I've wanted for a long time, but I can't justify it. Even if you don't think Seth will do anything he wasn't going to anyway, it's too much of a risk."

"Okay."

"Wait, you're just accepting my decision? I thought you were going to argue more."

He raised an eyebrow. "Do you want me to?"

I frowned. Did I? I wasn't sure. On the one hand, by not arguing he was respecting my opinion. On the other, a part of me wanted to be convinced that I could go, regardless of whether or not it was a good idea.

"Besides, I don't plan on leaving the compound yet," Heka said. "There's still time for you to change your mind."

"Ah, I see your plan." I moved one of my carved hound counters into the home space. "Your turn."

"I don't have a plan," he admitted. "And I didn't have instructions beyond asking you whether you'd return."

"That only makes your motivations more suspicious."

"Then you'll have to spend some more time with me so that I can reassure you of them."

"And so that we can have a rematch that you might win," I said as I moved my final hound into the home spot, winning the game.

"I can't promise that I'll win, but I'll accept the rematch."

An easy smile spread over my face in an expression I haven't felt this at ease around someone for a long time. I should have known the moment Heka turned up that he was going to make me feel things that I hadn't for a long time. Sometimes I suspected he really was magic.

CHAPTER 7

Avoiding Seth had turned out to be easier than I expected it to be, though I wasn't sure what that said about how involved with compound life I was. Perhaps I was deluded to think that Seth would notice if I left, he certainly barely noticed when I was around.

At least Heka noticed and seemed to want to be around me. It was nice to have someone in the compound who actually cared to see me.

I shook my head, trying to rid myself of thoughts of him. It was dangerous to let myself stray too far from the truth of how things were. Heka was here because he saw me as a challenge, nothing more.

Even as I thought it, I knew it was a lie. If he wasn't interested in more than that, then he wouldn't still be here, and I knew it.

Unfortunately, that only complicated things.

"Please see that I'm not disturbed," I said to the attendant outside the baths.

"Of course, Your Eminence." She dipped her head. "Do you want someone to attend you once you're inside?"

"No, thank you. I'll be fine on my own." Mostly because I felt like I needed time with my thoughts, and this was one of the only places where I could be certain Seth wouldn't come to find me. I had no idea why he stayed away, but I wasn't about to ask and stop him from respecting my space.

She nodded and allowed me to enter. Perhaps I should have asked her if there was anyone else inside.

The bathing pool waters smelled faintly of lotus blossoms and lapped against the sides softly. A selection of oils and soaps sat on the side for anybody to use. Some of them were ancient recipes, whereas others were more modern.

Despite having tried several of the modern hair treatments, I still preferred the older ones. Not only were they the same ones I'd been using my entire life, but they made my hair feel better. That wasn't something I could argue with.

I stripped off my clothes and folded them neatly, placing them on one of the benches at the side of the room.

The moment the water touched my skin, I started to relax. There was something about being under the water that made me forget about all of my worries and allowed me to focus just on the now.

I closed my eyes and leaned back against the side, staying in that position until I heard footsteps approaching.

"I thought I said not to be disturbed," I said without opening my eyes. While I was mildly annoyed at the imposition, I did my best to keep my feelings out of my voice.

"I thought you'd make an exception for me."

My eyes snapped open to see Heka standing at the side of the bath with an amused expression on his face.

"Do you mind if I join you?"

I blinked a few times, trying to process what he was asking but still too surprised that he'd appeared.

"I can go if you'd prefer."

"No, join me, there's plenty of room." I gestured to the rest of the bath. It had probably been built for a dozen people to use at once, and with just me in it, there was plenty of space.

His genuine smile reassured me that I'd done the right thing. He started to untie his robe, so I averted my gaze, not wanting to make him uncomfortable.

I didn't look back in his direction until I heard the water slosh as he sunk into the bath.

"How did you get in here?" I asked. "I told the attendant not to let anyone inside."

"I might have had my friend here..."

"Rhodopis?"

Shock flitted across his face.

"I'm not a fool, Heka," I reminded him.

He chuckled and pushed a hand through his dark hair, making it stand on end from the small amount of water he'd added to it. The gesture drew my attention to his bare chest, which probably wasn't something I should be staring at. His toned muscles and perfectly bronzed skin were impossible to ignore, even if I tried to.

"Nephthys?" he asked.

"Hmm?"

"You seemed lost in thought."

"Sorry. You were talking about Rhodopis."

"Ah, right, you wanted to know how I got in here, and then you got distracted by my chest," he teased.

"I did not." I crossed my arms, which pressed up my breasts and drew his attention there. "Now who's distracted."

He gave me a lopsided grin. "I'm not lying about staring."

"Fine, I was staring, are you happy?"

"A little." The tone in his voice revealed just how much he was enjoying this. "Anyway, I had Rhodopis tell the girl in front of the baths that she was needed elsewhere and then slipped inside. No one will disturb us now, though. You have me all to yourself for as much staring as you want."

"I doubt you came here to be objectified by me."

"To the compound, or to the baths?"

"Either."

"I'll give you the first one, but I can't swear to the second. What you don't seem to have realised is that I like being admired by you."

"Heka..."

"Am I not allowed to say it?" Somehow, he'd ended up moving a lot closer without me realising, and now we were barely a few inches apart.

I gulped. But not out of fear or discomfort. I like how close he's standing to me, it invokes feelings I haven't experienced in a long time. "It's dangerous to."

"So you do admire me?" His voice lowered so it was barely above a whisper, sending a small thrill through me.

"Yes." I was surprised my word was audible.

I bit my lip, drawing his attention down accidentally.

"Do you want me to kiss you?" he asked.

"You know the answer to that."

"I need to hear you say it," he responded.

Indecision warred within me. What I wanted and what I thought I could have were two different things and I wasn't sure how I could reconcile them.

But we were in the baths, with no one coming to disturb us. What was the harm in engaging in something I'd always wanted?

"Yes, you can kiss me."

It took him a moment for the words to register, but when they did, a genuine smile spread over his face.

"Are you sure?"

I nodded.

He didn't need any more encouraging than that. He closed the small gap between us and reached out to cup my cheek in his hand.

His gentle touch awakened feelings within me that I hadn't realised I still had.

My eyes fluttered closed as his lips met mine. I pressed myself against him, barely aware that we were naked. This wasn't the kind of kiss that made me think about being wrapped up in sheets during illicit trysts, it was the kind that made me think about intimate moments and someone who would always be by my side when I needed them to be.

It made me think I was special.

He deepened the kiss, putting a lot of unspoken emotions into the kiss. It was like he'd been waiting for this moment for thousands of years, though I knew that wasn't going to be true. Something about it felt right. Perhaps that was because of how many centuries it had been since anyone kissed me at all, but I doubted it.

Something about Heka fit with me, in a way Seth certainly never had.

We broke apart and I glanced down before realising I shouldn't be ashamed of what just happened. I looked up and met his gaze, seeing a similar jumble of emotions in his eyes.

"Now I know why you're the god of magic," I said before I could think twice about it.

Heka chuckled. "Is that what you're thinking about right now?"

My cheeks heated. "It sounded really bad out loud, didn't it?"

He reached out and tucked a strand of dark wet hair behind my ear. "No."

"Now you're lying."

"Maybe. But only so you'll let me kiss you again."

I shook my head in bemusement. "We need to be careful if we're going to do it again."

"If? So you're not going to pretend that nothing happened?"

"After a kiss like that, definitely not," I assured him. "I'm going to let it happen as many times as I safely can. In fact..." I trailed off and stepped forward, circling my arms around his neck.

He caught my drift and leaned in to kiss me again.

I knew it was reckless of us to carry on this way. And it could get dangerous if Seth got wind of anything going on. But it was worth it. Heka made me feel as if I was desirable. More than that, he made me feel like an actual person, not someone kept for appearance's sake and the power I theoretically had.

I wasn't about to let that slip through my fingers if I didn't have to.

CHAPTER 8

T he sun was already up, meaning it was later than Heka should be in my room. But there wasn't anything I could do about it now. My attendants knew better than to disturb me, and I suspected that several of them had worked out that I'd taken a lover, but so long as they didn't tell anyone or figure out who he really was, I didn't think it would matter.

"The longer you stay, the more dangerous it's going to be for you," I warned him, like I'd started to do every morning. As much as I wanted him to stay for as long as possible, I wasn't foolish enough to think that was a good idea. It was dangerous.

He took my hand in his and laid it on his chest. I nestled my head against his shoulder.

"I don't want to leave without you," he admitted.

I sighed. "But why?"

"Because you deserve to be happy. I know we haven't seen one another in a few thousand years, but I'll never forget the way you used to be overshadowed by what everyone else needed. It's time for you to actually be happy."

"I never thought anyone noticed me."

"I did," he assured me. "And even then, I wanted to do something about it."

"At least you've done something about it now," I joked.

He let out a small laugh. "Even so, it's hard to believe that I'm in your bed."

"Because of Seth?"

He sighed. "You never stop thinking about him, do you?"

"Not in the way you think. I don't love him, I never did. Not like that, anyway," I said hurriedly.

"I know," he assured me. "Everyone knew. I think that's one of the reasons they're all so confused that you never came back to Karnak."

"It's hard to explain," I admitted. "At first, I didn't realise what was happening. Then for a short time I was angry at Isis and Osiris for forcing Seth into a difficult position with Horus. After that, I felt isolated and too embarrassed to return. Eventually, it turned into me wanting to help Seth become more like the person he used to be, before all of this happened."

"And then it became habit?"

I shook my head. "And then he became dangerous. Seth knows how to kill me." I waited for his surprise, but it didn't come. "You already know."

"That we can all be killed? Yes, I know. Not everyone does though."

"I don't think it's the kind of information we should be keeping from the younger gods," I admitted.

"Perhaps not, but that was the promise you all made when I didn't have any say in it, so that's what you need to stick to. How did Seth find out how to kill you?"

"You're going to think I'm an idiot, but I told him. I had to do something so he'd believe I could be trusted and for some reason I thought the best way was to reveal my biggest secret. It was foolish, I know. He'd never have guessed if I hadn't said anything."

It was one of the biggest secrets at Karnak. All gods could die, but the way it could happen was different for each of us. An odd failsafe in our design that both protected us and made us vulnerable. Many of the younger gods had no idea, and none of the humans or demis knew at all.

"Is it something he can do from afar?" Heka asked.

I shook my head. "We'd need to be in the same room."

"Then come to Karnak, you won't have anything to worry about once you're there."

I grimaced. "And if he catches me? I've always assumed that was when he'd do it the moment he found me. I doubt he has any affection for me at all."

"You don't know that." From the tone in his voice it was clear that he didn't think I was wrong.

"It's not something I'm in any hurry to test."

"We'll be able to protect you if you're at Karnak," Heka assured me.

"Perhaps."

"What can I do to convince you?" he asked.

I let out a loud sigh. "Nothing. I'm sorry, but I can't leave with you, even if I want to."

He nodded, seeming to be resigned to what I was saying. Somehow, I didn't think I'd heard the last of this.

Before either of us could say anything else, a knock sounded on my door.

"Your Eminence, your presence is needed," one of my attendants said. "I'm just going to get your clothing and I'll be back to dress you."

I exchanged a panicked look with Heka. "This is why you were supposed to leave before dawn."

"I tried, but you distracted me," he pointed out.

I got to my feet, trying my best to ignore the way his gaze followed me. "You need to hide. You can sneak out once I'm gone." I grabbed a robe from the foot of my bed and wrapped it around myself.

He nodded and finally got out of bed and grabbed his clothes before climbing under the bed.

I raised an eyebrow. "Really?"

"There isn't exactly anywhere else to hide," he pointed out.

I gnawed on my bottom lip. He wasn't wrong about that. My rooms hadn't been built with the intention of anyone being able to hide in it.

The door opened, chasing all thoughts of where it might be better to hide out of my mind.

A petite woman with braided dark brown hair entered my room with a freshly pressed dress over her arm.

"You're new, aren't you?" I asked the attendant without thinking about it. I was focusing too hard on whether or not I could hear Heka breathing from under the bed.

"Yes, Your Eminence, my name is Leila." She smiled so sweetly that it almost broke my heart.

She was too pretty to last long-serving me. I knew some of the more experienced slaves sent the pretty newcomers to places where they knew they wouldn't be mistreated, and hopefully would be out of the way of Seth, but it rarely worked forever. I'd do what I could to keep her safe, but I was starting to understand how limited my power actually was. Especially here.

"You said that I'd been summoned?" I asked her as she set down the dress and started getting other items ready. My clothing might leave my chambers, but my jewels did not.

"Erm, your presence is required," she said.

"What does that mean?" Dread filled me as I considered the possibilities.

"The Emperor wants to see you."

I closed my eyes and took a deep breath. I knew it was going to be him. No one else in the compound would want to see me. Or at least none I could think of.

"He's outside," she said.

"Ah. I see." My blood turned cold within me, but I knew enough that I had to keep going through the motions as if it hadn't.

Seth was outside my room and Heka was hidden under my bed having spent the night in it.

Though that part wasn't the most worrying thing about his presence. Seth had no idea he was in the compound at all, and I didn't want to think about what might happen if he found out. If a god defected from Karnak, the first place they went was to Seth, not to me. There'd be no hiding the truth.

"You should go, Leila," I said having regained some composure. "I can get ready on my own."

She hesitated for a moment, unsure what to do. I could understand that. She'd been instructed to help me get ready for my day, and here I was basically telling her not to.

"You won't get in trouble," I promised. "You're just doing as I ask."

She opened her mouth as if to say something, but stopped in her tracks with her eyes wide.

I turned slowly so I was facing the door, unsurprised to see Seth standing there with his normal scowl marring his features. He could be a handsome man if he used some more pleasant facial expressions.

"I'll be with you in a moment," I said tersely.

"I've been waiting long enough, Nephthys," he sneered.

"I'll be with you once I've gotten dressed," I said more firmly than before.

"It's no matter, I don't intend to be here long." He moved into the room.

I stepped in front of Leila so I could shield her from view. Seth's anger seemed to be aimed at me, but it was better if I didn't give him an obvious outlet for it.

As hard as it was to resist pulling my robe tighter around me, I managed. I didn't want Seth to know how uncomfortable he made me.

"What did you come here for?"

"Is that any way to talk to your emperor?" he demanded.

"When he insists on barging into my private chambers, it is, yes." I should have just said sorry, but I couldn't shake the thought of Heka hiding under the bed and hearing every word. I didn't want him to know just how scared I was of Seth.

"You haven't been in the dining hall for the past three days."

"No, I haven't."

"That will change."

"I will come to the dining hall when I wish to," I said through gritted teeth.

Seth stepped forward so we were almost touching. My whole body tensed, a completely different reaction it had to when Heka was standing so close. "You may not be my wife in private, but as far as the rest of the world is concerned you are, and you will act as such," he seethed.

I glared at him, hating the way he was ordering me about, but knowing there was nothing I could do about it.

"I expect you to be there tonight," he demanded. "If you're not, there will be consequences."

A shiver ran down my spine. I had no doubt that he was telling the truth about that.

Seth didn't wait for my reply and stormed out of the room, slamming the door behind him.

"Leave me," I commanded Leila, trying to hide the fact my voice was shaking as I said the words.

"Of course, Your Eminence. If you need assistance, I'll be outside." She dipped her head and left the room.

Every part of me was on edge in the way only Seth could manage.

That was close. I glanced towards where Heka was already climbing out from under the bed. Somehow, I had to convince him to leave Seth's compound. It wasn't safe for him here.

"Nephthys, are you okay?" he asked.

"You have to leave." My voice shook. This had been far from my worst interaction with Seth, but I knew what he was capable of. I was a fool to think I could carry on spending my nights with Heka while keeping it a secret and keeping him safe.

"All right, but I'll be back later..."

"Not the room. The compound." I glanced away from him, unable to look at him without tears stinging my eyes. I didn't want him to see how upset this was all making me.

"Nephthys..." He reached out for me but I stepped away.

"Please, Heka. It isn't safe. You have to go."

"I can't."

"Of course you can. You know how to get in and out of the compound, just leave the same way you got in." Tears rolled down my cheeks. I wiped them away, but they were only replaced with more. It had been a long time since I'd cried but my emotions had decided it was time to betray me.

"I don't mean that I can't physically leave." His voice was softer than I expected it to be. "How can I disappear back to the safety of Karnak knowing that you're here having to do the whim of a man you don't even like."

I grimaced. When he put it like that, I sounded a bit like a fool. It wasn't the first time Seth's actions had made me feel that way.

"I can't explain it," I mumbled.

"I know." Heka reached out and pulled me into his arms.

For a moment, I thought about resisting, but that wasn't going to help anyone. I wrapped my arms tightly around him and leaned against his chest. The action seemed to unlock a flood gate within me and I sobbed loudly.

My heart was torn between what it wanted and what it feared.

Heka didn't say a word, he just stood there and stroked my hair, holding me tightly and giving me the comfort and support I so desperately needed.

CHAPTER 9

Stepping outside my rooms for the first evening in a few days revealed the truth about the status of things in the compound. The tension was everywhere and I could tell from the way everyone was moving around that they thought something bad was going to happen.

Was this a new thing, or had I just been blind to what was truly going on? I didn't think I'd want the answer to that question.

I tried to keep a smile on my face as I made my way through the compound towards the banquet hall, just like Seth wanted.

A small part of me loathed myself for being so weak and giving in to what he wanted, but I knew it was best for everyone's safety.

A loud shout cut through the air, calling the attention of everyone in the vicinity. I quickened my pace, my heart pounding. What if Seth had found out about Heka? Or any of the other spies in the compound. Both would make him angry beyond belief and someone would pay the price. While I doubted he knew how to kill Heka, he'd still be able to hurt him.

I entered the main courtyard outside the banquet hall to find a small crowd had formed. While some of those closer to Seth seemed to be enjoying themselves, most of those assembled seemed to be a mixture of scared and repulsed.

Seth stood in the middle with his hand outstretched for his foreman to place a whip there.

My stomach tied into knots. A young boy lay on the ground in front of him, quivering in fear.

I looked to the side to find Rhodopis standing beside me, her shoulders tense with the pressure. No doubt she was thinking about her friend who had suffered at Seth's hands.

"What happened?" I asked.

"I don't know," she responded quietly. "Probably nothing. And certainly not something that deserves this." Disgust came through her every word.

A woman rushed forward and tried to step towards the boy, but one of the others caught hold of her and pulled her back. "You can't."

"But..."

"You know what will happen if someone interferes. You'll make it worse for him," her companion said.

I grimaced at the truth. No one could stop Seth once he'd started. He'd turn his wrath on anyone that tried and they'd probably end up dead.

Except that wasn't true. There were exceptions. And I was one of them.

I stepped forward, only for Rhodopis to reach out and stop me.

"Nephthys, no," she whispered.

"Let me."

She searched my face and must have seen something that made it clear I wasn't about to change my mind about this as she ended up just nodding.

"What's his name?"

"Tye. But..."

"Send his mother to get him as soon as Seth is distracted, please."

I didn't wait for her to confirm my request, I knew she'd do it.

I strode into the middle of the courtyard. My heart pounded in my ears but my anger outweighed my fear. I'd turned a blind eye to the things Seth was doing here for too long, and it was time that ended.

"Tye, there you are," I said as loudly as possible. "Would you fetch me my fan from my room, please?"

I ignored the shocked murmuring coming from those assembled and focused on Seth's expression. His emotions flashed across his face, more obvious than he wanted them to be.

"Nephthys, what are you doing?"

"I need my fan and I asked Tye to get it for me. Is that a problem?"

Anger flared in his eyes, but it was nothing compared to the simmering heat inside me. One thing Seth never considered was the enemies his temper was making him. Or that they could be more dangerous than him as a result.

"I am disciplining him." He toyed with the coiled whip in his hands.

"For what?"

"He didn't show me the proper respect." Seth uncoiled the whip, his focus solely on me. I didn't think he'd dare to use it on me, but I readied myself just in case.

Tye cried out and I glanced around in time to find his mother helping him to his feet. He held his arm close to his chest as if it was injured, causing another wave of anger to head through me.

The crack of the whip sounded against the ground next to them as Seth grew impatient of waiting.

I turned back to him, anger flaring so hard inside me that my wings erupted from my back. They stretched out wide, effectively shielding Tye and his mother from Seth's view.

"Put the whip away, Seth." The anger caused my voice to get low and darkness to swirl within me. This part of me was always there, but normally stayed hidden deep within. It certainly had for the past few years while I'd been checked out from everything going on around me. I was only just starting to realise how wrong of me that was.

"You don't know what you're doing," he hissed at me. "That boy..."

"Is a child," I finished for him. "You were going to whip a child for no reason other than your falsely wounded pride."

Silence reigned throughout the courtyard as people waited to see how this would go.

Seth stepped closer to me, but unlike in my bedroom, I was determined not to back down and act scared this time.

"You forget your place, Nephthys."

"And you forget yours. You're not the god you used to be."

Shock flitted across his face. No doubt he hadn't expected anyone to say that to him.

I took it as my chance to leave and spun around. The worst he could do was attack me, and that wasn't going to do any permanent damage.

Tye and his mother were nowhere to be seen. It would probably be best if I found somewhere for them to disappear to, though where that could be, I wasn't sure.

I ignored everyone as I walked away and back towards my rooms. I didn't want to make it seem as if I was in league with someone and have Seth take out his anger on them instead of me. It was better if he thought I was acting alone and didn't have any allies. I didn't know what would happen otherwise, but I could be certain that it wouldn't be good.

It was only once I was away from everyone that what I'd done sunk in. I retracted my wings and ducked into a small alcove to try and steady my erratic breathing. I was a fool if I thought this wasn't going to have consequences, and not just for Tye and his mother, but also for me. Seth wasn't going to let this go unpunished.

Someone approached, and every muscle in my body tensed as I waited for some kind of attack.

"It's just me," Rhodopis whispered. "Are you all right?"

A small part of me wanted to lie to her and say yes, but I knew she'd see through that. She was a perceptive person, that was part of what made her so useful as a spy.

"No. What did I just do?"

"Something wonderful and awful all at the same time," she answered. "But I think you already knew that."

I smiled weakly. "That's one way of putting it. But it's going to cause a problem now."

"Yes, it probably is," she agreed. "But Heka said you'd been invited back to Karnak, perhaps you should take him up on the offer?"

"So you're not even going to pretend you aren't Karnak's spy anymore?" I asked.

"I think you're too intelligent to fall for it if I did," she pointed out.

"How long?"

"Do you remember when Ra and his cohort visited?"

I raised an eyebrow. "That's a while."

"It's easy to slip under the radar when no one pays any attention to you to begin with."

"You should come with us," I said. "Back to Karnak."

She shook her head. "No one suspects me. I can stay here and help more."

"What about Tye and his mother? Do you think they'll come?"

"I don't know," she admitted. "But I'll ask."

"Thank you. Can you get a message to Heka to meet me in my rooms?" I wasn't sure if that was the safest thing to do, but I'd need to go there and act normally until the last possible moment or I'd raise suspicion.

Rhodopis nodded. "But I don't think I'll need to. I suspect he'll already be there waiting for you."

Perhaps she was right, but I wanted to make sure he was all right with my own eyes. And then we'd leave the compound behind us.

I doubted I'd ever be coming back.

CHAPTER 10

Nerves jittered in my stomach. They'd been my constant companions ever since I'd returned to my rooms and realised I had to wait until nightfall to do anything. At least it would if we wanted to give ourselves the most time possible to get away.

"Are you ready?" Heka asked.

"Saying no isn't going to change the fact we need to go," I pointed out.

"It doesn't, no."

"Then I guess my answer to that question doesn't matter." I looked around my room and waited for a sense of sadness or regret to sink in, but nothing did. This place hadn't been home to me in a long time. Perhaps it never had been.

"All right, let's get this over with. The sooner we leave, the sooner we get the dangerous part out of the way."

"I thought you said it was going to be dangerous no matter what?"

I sighed. "That was before I was an idiot."

"Hey, you weren't an idiot," he said, turning me around and pulling me close. "You were brave."

I leaned into him. "I should have done it sooner. I shouldn't have let Seth get away with the things he's been doing for so long."

"Maybe not, but no one else was stopping him either. And you said yourself that he knows how to kill you. Even if he never said as much, he was holding that over your head."

"I just wish I hadn't been so weak."

"Nephthys, listen to me. It's okay to have made a mistake. Do you think people are going to be in their homes tonight lamenting all the times you haven't done anything, or do you think they'll be talking about the time you did? And next time Seth brings out his whip, maybe someone else will have the courage to stand up and say no."

"Shouldn't I stay so that I can make sure that happens?" I whispered.

"I think that depends. Do you want to stay and do you think that it's safe to say?"

"No. To both."

"Then there's more you can do for the people living in this compound from the safety of Karnak. Think of all the information you can tell the others about the layout of the buildings, which gods are here, and where the weaknesses are. They can only get so much information from spies, you've had access to so much more."

"But I've not been privy to most of Seth's plans."

"Maybe not, but you still know a lot more than Rhodopis does just because of who you are."

I nodded. "I know you're right, I'm just scared."

"Of?"

"Leaving, staying, and everything in between."

Heka chuckled dryly. "I can see how that might be confusing."

"Exactly." I sighed. "But I also know that we need to go and that it has to be now." I gestured to the small window that revealed the darkening sky.

"Everyone should be at the evening meal, and I doubt Seth will think twice about me not being there considering how it will remind everyone of what I did."

He nodded. "Have you got everything?"

"I think so."

"Your bag isn't very big."

"We're making a quick getaway, I didn't think a trunk full of unnecessary things would be a good idea. These are just some sentimental pieces I'd rather not leave behind." Most of it was jewellery from my sister and mother.

"Ah, right. Then let's go."

"Are we meeting Tye and his mother?" I asked.

Sadness flickered through Heka's eyes. "They're not coming."

"Oh." I was sure they'd have their reasons, but I couldn't help feeling a little disappointed about that. I'd have thought they'd have leapt at a chance to escape the compound.

But I couldn't dwell on it. Staying could mean a death sentence for me. And after I'd finally found my voice again, I didn't want that. I needed a chance to make a difference, and Heka was right that the way to do that was to get back to Karnak and tell them what I knew.

Heka checked that the coast was clear before making his way out of my rooms. I followed behind, both glad and worried to be out in the open air.

Neither of us said anything as we made our way through the twists and turns of the compound. While he didn't say as much, I suspected Rhodopis had shown him the best way to get to the door closest to the oasis. I certainly hoped so, as I had no idea of the best way even if I wanted one.

Other than almost crossing paths with a few guards, we didn't seem to be having any trouble. Though perhaps that was a trick to catch us out.

No. I had to stop thinking like that. Technically, no one had to know that I was escaping even if we ran into them, and so long as they had no idea who Heka was or recognise him as the god of magic, we wouldn't have any problems.

I didn't relax until the door came into view. This was where we were trying to get to. Once we were outside the walls, there should be a lot less risk.

"I'll check the coast is clear on the outside," Heka said. "Wait here until I get back."

I nodded, though I didn't like the idea of us ending up separated.

He hurried over to the door and pushed it open, stepping through and out of sight.

Every sound had me on edge and searching for the source of it.

When the door finally cracked open, I let out a sigh of relief. I could get through and to safety. I knew there was more of a journey to come before we were truly away from here, but I wasn't going to dwell on that.

I hurried over, determined to put this place behind me.

A hand reached out and grabbed hold of my arm. I let out a small shriek before looking back and finding a panicked looking Amun behind me.

"Don't tell Karnak I'm here," he whispered urgently.

"Do you really think they don't know?"

"I've made it so they don't," he assured me. "Please promise you won't change that."

I considered for a moment. Why wouldn't he want Karnak to know? As far as I knew, he wasn't a double agent, and he'd spent most of his time at the compound anyway. "I won't lie if someone asks me directly, but I won't tell them of my own free will," I promised. "On one condition."

He raised an eyebrow. "Are you really in a position to bargain?"

"You wouldn't be asking me to lie for you if you didn't think I was," I pointed out.

Amun sighed. "Fine, what do you want me to do?"

"Protect as many people as you can from Seth's cruelty."

He raised an eyebrow. "You might as well ask me to save the world."

"Perhaps. But that's not what I want you to promise."

He sighed. "Fine. I'll do what I can without raising suspicions."

That was easier than I expected it to be, and tracked with what I'd experienced of Amun so far anyway. It still didn't make much sense that he was here, but I knew he had to have his reasons. I wouldn't be surprised if I found him back at Karnak in a few months time.

"Thank you."

"Likewise. Good luck with your journey." He let go of my arm and disappeared back into the compound.

"What was all of that about?" Heka asked from his position waiting by the door. I was glad he'd been here to witness Amun's strange request or I'd have thought that it was all in my head.

"I have no idea." I glanced in the direction the other god had headed in, but he'd already disappeared. "But let's go before anyone else turns up. I don't think the next person is going to be as understanding about the fact we're leaving."

"The coast is clear on this side."

"All right, then let's go."

I took a deep breath and stepped over the threshold. I didn't let it go until the door had closed, shutting us off from the compound inside.

This was it. I was leaving the compound, and this time I wasn't going to be coming back.

CHAPTER 11

A wave of affection and longing flooded through me at the sight of Karnak temple rising out of the sands, a beacon of hope in my otherwise dark life. A small part of me didn't believe I was standing in front of it and that this was a dream that had been sent in order to torture me.

But that wasn't true. I was here.

Home.

The word almost felt foreign.

Heka slipped his hand into mine and gave it a squeeze. "How does it feel to see it again?"

"Like nothing has changed."

He chuckled. "Then you're in a for a rude awakening. Part of the temple is now open to human tourists. They have no idea that gods still live in the other half."

"Considering the alternative, I think I can accept that."

I didn't let go of his hand as we made our way across the sands. The warm mid-morning sun felt better on my skin than it did back at the compound, but I knew that was all in my head.

"Do you think Tye and his mother are okay?"

Heka nodded. "I gave Rhodopis a spell that would conceal their identities until it's all blown over."

"But they didn't want to leave?"

"No. Their family has always been at the compound and they didn't want to leave them behind. I can understand it."

"I can't."

"Why not? You stayed much longer than you were actually happy."

I let out a loud sigh. "I suppose, but I feel more than a little foolish for staying as long as I did. And I feel guilty for leaving everybody else behind."

"You can do more about the people still at the compound from Karnak than you can from your rooms there," Heka pointed out. "Now you're here, you can fight for them. You'd probably even be able to bargain with Ma'at for information."

"I don't think she'll appreciate me withholding things."

"And yet you're going to stay silent about Amun, aren't you?"

I sighed. "I don't know. I want to keep my promise to him, but at the same time, I don't want to lie to anyone. It's going to be hard enough getting them all to trust me again after I've spent so long at Seth's compound."

"They'll trust you."

I threw him an incredulous look. "Perhaps you will, and my family, but I doubt many of the others will. They'll be convinced that I'm still on Seth's side, that I'm his wife through and through."

"Then we'll have to do everything we can to convince them otherwise."

I smiled uneasily. I hoped there was truth in his words, but somehow, I doubted it. Most of the gods had switched sides at one point or another during Seth and Ma'at's conflict, but most hadn't stayed on Seth's side for as long as I had.

"And if you manage to convince Ma'at, then everyone else will have to fall into place. She has the final say about everything."

"As she always has," I muttered. "I know my father was the Pharaoh at some point, but it's always felt as if Ma'at was really the one in charge."

"I don't think you're wrong," Heka agreed. "But at least now we're admitting she's pulling the strings. It's probably why Atum is nowhere to be seen."

"He's missing?"

"I wouldn't go that far. He's sulking on his mountain because he's not important anymore and thinks that we should all be worshipping him instead of the humans so he can regain his power."

"That's some ego."

"Mmhmm. He's not the only one acting strangely. Horus barely visits Karnak, he just stays in his temple. They say that Khonsu is pretending to be a wise woman in one city or another, and

Hathor barely pays any attention to what's going on."

"It sounds as if Seth's going to be the one winning this battle," I observed.

"Perhaps. But I wouldn't make any bets on it just yet. I'm sure Ma'at has a plan."

"Hmm." He seemed to be putting a lot of faith in the goddess of truth and justice. Ma'at was powerful and intelligent, but she hadn't managed to put a stop to the endless conflict yet.

Our conversation was cut short by our arrival at the entrance to the temple. Priests and priestesses milled around doing their own thing that kept the place running. Unlike the slaves at Seth's compound, these demi-gods were free to serve the gods they chose, and live the lives they wanted to. If they wished to leave temple service, they would be able to. Even with only a brief glance into their lives, I could see how much better they were for that difference.

Two figures caught my attention from between the demi-gods and a giddy lightness filled me. A part of me that I thought had long gone reappeared and I rushed towards them, dodging between people and leaving Heka to follow.

The first woman was unmistakable even from a distance. With her dark blue skin peppered with glittering stars, the woman I thought of as my mother was recognisable to anyone. Like all of the other gods, we didn't share genetics or a bloodline, but she was the one who birthed me and raised me.

And next to her was my sister, Isis. Like Nut, she didn't share any actual blood with me, but that was the way I saw it.

She opened her arms to me and enveloped me in a tight embrace. Nut stepped forward and wrapped her arms around us both. Happiness bubbled away within me and a small trail of tears rolled down my cheeks.

We broke apart and I studied them both in more detail through the veil of tears. Neither of them had changed much in the years we'd spent apart, and I imagined that was the same for me. But we'd all changed on the inside.

"I'm so happy to be home." My voice cracked from the emotion.

"We're glad you're back, darling," Nut said with a warm smile. "We've missed you."

"I'm sorry I didn't come sooner. I should have done." I should never have left Karnak in the first place. I couldn't believe I'd let Seth take me away from my family. Or that I'd let him keep me away from them.

"Why don't you come inside, we'll see that you and Heka get some refreshments," Nut said.

"I'm sorry that there isn't a formal reception for you," Isis added as she slipped her arm through mine the way we used to do when we were younger and visiting the various festivals and events throughout the land. "I wasn't sure how some people were going to react to you being back and we thought it might be better to reintroduce you more gradually."

"You've not got any less blunt over the years," I observed.

She chuckled. "If you listen to Osiris, I've gotten more so."

I glanced over my shoulder to make sure Heka was following us. He smiled reassuringly, probably having guessed that I was glad to see my family again. His understanding and acceptance that there was more to my life than our relationship was just another way in which he was different from Seth.

A small part of me regretted that I'd wasted so much of my life on Seth and his vendetta. But there was no point dwelling on it so long as I made sure things were different going forward. Heka was part of that.

Isis and Nut led me inside the temple, walking slowly enough for me to take everything in. It was almost like stepping back in time, and yet in many ways, it wasn't. Things had changed a bit, but not as much as the reports I'd heard suggested the outside world had.

It only enforced my sensation of being home.

We passed several other gods, some of whom didn't give me a second glance, but others shot me dirty looks. It seemed that not everyone was happy about my return.

It didn't matter. Right now I was going to focus on catching up with my family and the other people I'd missed while I'd been away. Once I'd done that, I could focus on changing other people's minds. As Heka said, I knew information they wanted. I wasn't going to swap it for approval, but if I gained some because of it, I wasn't going to complain.

Chapter 12

The atmosphere in the banquet hall was completely different to how it felt when there was a big meal at the compound. People laughed and joked with one another, not seeming to care that they might cause an offence they wouldn't be able to cover up.

No doubt there were problems between individual gods here at Karnak still. I couldn't help but notice a lot of people were giving Ra a wide berth. He'd always had a reputation for being ruthless in his pursuit of what he thought was right, sometimes that created unintentional enemies.

"It's so different," I said to Heka. "Who is that talking to Ma'at?" I asked.

"Oh, that's Edrice, she used to be a priestess but recently got promoted to become a goddess in the Hall of Judgement."

I raised an eyebrow.

"She wasn't replacing you."

"That wasn't going to be my question. I didn't think it was possible to promote people to goddesses."

"Apparently Ma'at found a way. I've talked to Edrice, she's definitely a goddess."

"Is that what happened to Rhodopis too?"

"Ah, so she does know."

"That she's a goddess? Yes, she told me the night I snuck out to meet you at the oasis."

"Interesting, I assumed she had no idea. I didn't know anything about her other than what code word she'd use when we could meet up. From what I can tell, she was born a goddess, just like you were."

"You can really tell that?" While our paths had crossed before he'd arrived at Seth's compound, I'd never had much of a chance to ask him about how his powers worked. Nor would I have if the opportunity had arisen. A god's magic was something private. Not to mention the fluidity most of us had when it came to it. If a human believed we were the god or goddess of something, then we gained powers related to that. It didn't matter if we were already the god or goddess of something.

"I can. But not in as much depth as I used to be able to."

"Ah, the effects of the world forgetting us."

"Indeed."

Our conversation was cut short by Isis coming to take a seat beside us. She gestured for one of the servants to bring her a goblet of wine and smiled her thanks at them.

"How are you settling back in?" she asked.

"Okay, I think. Heka is letting me stay in his temple until mine is ready again."

"We'd have had it ready for you if we'd known you were coming." She shot him a disapproving look.

"It wasn't Heka's fault," I said, not wanting her to think he'd done anything wrong or against the plan. "I did something foolish and we had to leave in a hurry."

"She didn't do anything foolish," Heka contradicted. "She did something very brave."

I glanced down, not wanting Isis to see the slight embarrassment on my face.

"I did something that I'm ashamed I didn't do sooner," I admitted. "I should have stood up to Seth a long time ago."

"We all understand why you didn't," she assured me. "No one blames you for it."

I let out a soft snort. "Are you sure about that? Because I don't think the others got the memo." I waved my hand around the room. While some of the gods and goddesses were acknowledging me, others were ignoring me completely. I supposed in some ways that was better than having to justify myself and my decisions constantly.

"It'll take time, but they'll come around," Isis promised. "Especially when they realise Ma'at is on your side."

I raised an eyebrow. "Is she?"

Isis chuckled. "I'll admit she has a strange way of showing it sometimes, but yes, she is. She wants to see you tomorrow."

"If you two will excuse me, Ptah is asking for me," Heka said. He leaned in and kissed my cheek, before nodding to Isis.

I watched him leave, longing for his presence beside me again.

"Do you think Ma'at can pronounce me as officially divorced?" I asked.

"You are already," Isis pointed out. "You moved out of Seth's compound, nobody here is going to argue with that."

"Seth would."

"We can send him an official message stating your marriage is over if you want, but I don't see what difference it'll make."

"Probably none," I admitted. "But he's changed, Isis. Even more than you think he has. It's like the part of him that knows how to care about people has disappeared completely. I still don't understand what happened."

"I don't think any of us do," she agreed. "Osiris often wonders if it was something he did."

"Seth never told me. But that's not a surprise. I've never had the relationship with Seth that you have with Osiris. You actually talk to one another."

"It wasn't always like that."

"Oh right, you had about a year where you barely talked after you got married, and then you fell madly in love and have stayed that way for thousands of years." I smiled to show her that I was only meaning it in a sisterly way. I was happy for them both.

"When you put it like that you may have a point." But it looks like you've found someone completely different now." She nodded over in Heka's direction.

He caught us looking and gave us a small wave.

A wide smile spread over my face.

"Aha, so I did read that situation right," Isis said triumphantly.

"We weren't doing a lot to hide it," I pointed out. "I'm staying in his temple, remember? What do you think we're doing there?"

She raised her eyebrows. "You were brave to start something under Seth's nose. He isn't exactly known for being rational when he's jealous."

"You know as well as I do that Seth has never been jealous as far as I'm concerned. Or if he has, his jealousy comes from wanting to possess and control, not because of me. He didn't even notice Heka was in the compound."

"He always did miss things right under his nose." There was a hint of sadness in her voice that I understood well. The love of his family was something Seth never understood that he had.

"And I'm glad of it. I have no idea what he'd do if he'd found out."

"But that wasn't enough to stop you."

"It's bad, I know..."

"No, Neph, it isn't."

Hearing her use the childhood endearment she'd given me made my heart swell up several times.

"Sometimes, the way we feel about someone is so strong that we can't ignore it. I suspect that's how you feel about Heka. To be honest, I thought something was going to happen between the two of you a long time ago," she said.

"I always thought he was attractive," I admitted, knowing that it was safe to talk to her like this. "And intelligent. I do like that in a man."

"And yet you settled for Seth."

I chuckled. "You know there was no settling involved. I was pressured into that."

"Not by us. We never wanted that for you."

"I know. But I felt like I owed the humans who believed in us to be paired and married. You know what it was like, you married Osiris for the same reason, it just turned out better in the end for you."

"Ah the follies of youth."

"That's one way of putting it. I just wished I'd grown wiser about it before now. I spent a long time not doing anything about my mistakes."

"That doesn't matter," Isis assured me. "Everyone here has done something wrong at some point. We forgive them and we get on with our lives. They'll do the same for you."

"Eventually."

"It'll only take until the next big thing happens," she assured me. "And having a relationship with Heka will help. A lot of people here respect him."

"With good reason."

"And then you'll have Ma'at's approval, and you'll let everyone know more about what's going on in Seth's compound. They'll be eating out of your hand by the end of the week."

I let out a small amused laugh at my sister's prediction. "Somehow, I doubt that. But I don't need adoration. I just want to be away from the tension surrounding Seth's compound. I didn't realise how bad it was until I got here."

"Then the important thing is that you're here, you're safe, and you're home. Nothing else matters."

I leaned back in my seat and picked up my goblet of wine. I took a sip and let it all sink in. Isis was right. I was safe and I was home. It might take the other gods some time to accept me, but that was fine by me. Time was a luxury I had now.

CHAPTER 13

Heka slipped his hand into mine and swung it back and forth as if we were young lovesick gods. The soft breeze of the night air and the croak of frogs coming from the sacred lake only helped add to the ambience.

I closed my eyes and took in a lungful of air, enjoying the way freedom smelled. It was silly to think it was any different from the air back at the compound. But then, it wasn't the air that had actually changed, it was me. At Karnak, I got to be my own person. All I had to do was rediscover who that was.

"I'm sorry your temple isn't ready," Heka said.

"Don't be. You had no idea we'd be leaving in such a hurry."

"I'd hoped I'd be able to send word ahead, yes."

"Then it's my fault that it's not ready, not yours," I pointed out.

He drew us towards a carved stone bench and motioned for me to sit.

I did and made sure I pulled him to sit down next to me

"I don't think it's really your fault," he countered.

"Then it's nobody's fault. Besides, I like sharing a room with you." I leaned in and kissed his cheek.

"I can't say I'm complaining about it." He grinned wickedly. "Though perhaps when you reopen your temple you could ask for them to supply a bigger bed, I don't think mine was made for two."

"Then you're in luck. Mine was." Not that it was ever used for anyone other than me. "I have a private bathing room too, I can get one of my priestesses to prepare it."

"You have priestesses here?" he asked.

I grimaced. "Not yet, they've all been tending to my other temples. I've recalled a few of them to

Karnak, but I dread to think what they're going to tell me about the state of them. I'm surprised I still have standing temples given that I all but abandoned them."

Heka frowned. "Did Seth not let you tend to your own temple business?"

"Definitely not. He thought it would split my focus away from his agenda."

"But he didn't seem to care what you did within the compound."

I laughed bitterly. "Seth isn't the most logical of people. In his mind, me doing nothing was better than me tending to my own temples. I suppose he was worried that I'd remember how powerful I could be and would stop supporting him."

"Except that you did stop."

"And that won't be the last of his theories or plans to backfire on him," I pointed out. "Seth's success rate isn't particularly great."

"That's true."

"But can we stop talking about him? I'm going to have to do it during my meeting with Ma'at tomorrow and I don't want to spend the rest of tonight talking about my ex-husband too."

Ah, ex-husband. It sounded so good to say it out loud. Things had been over between us in my head for a long time, and I suspected Seth felt the same way, he just didn't want to let me go either.

"I'm sorry, I should have thought about that."

I reached out and took his hand in mine, giving it a squeeze. "It's okay, I'm not mad about it."

He smiled reassuringly at me to show me that he wasn't either. That was what I liked about being around Heka. He didn't make me feel as if I had to be any less than I really am.

"I like being able to show you affection in public here," I admitted, lifting up our hands to show exactly what I was talking about. "Unless that's not something you want, in which case I can stop."

"Why would I want you to stop?"

I sighed. "I'm not sure. Maybe you think I'll taint your image because of who I am and where I came from before I returned to Karnak? You know, even now I'm saying it, I don't think it makes much sense."

"It does to me. You've been told for so long what your worth was that you were in Seth's compound, and now you're not, it's natural to be confused about where that leaves you."

I sighed. "I hate that you're right."

"I know. But it'll fade in time. And even when it does I'm going to keep showing you just how much I want to be seen with you. One of the hardest things about being in the compound was that I couldn't show you how much you mean to me in public. And now I can do that and it doesn't matter who sees."

"You don't mind?" Hope blossomed in my voice.

"No, I don't mind," he promised. "I want to be with you, Nephthys. Not because of what you represent or the power you have, I want to be with you because of you."

My heart swelled uncontrollably within me. I hadn't felt like this since I was in my twenties and experienced my first relationship.

Heka reached out and tucked a strand of hair behind my ear.

"Can I kiss you?" he asked.

"You know you can."

"I know, but I felt like this was the right time to ask again." The adoration shining through his eyes was even brighter than the reflection of the moon in the water. And it was all for me.

I closed my eyes as he leaned in and pressed his lips against mine. I circled my arms around his neck and pushed myself against him, kissing him back with everything I had. I needed him to know that now we were in Karnak, I wanted him just as much. It had nothing to do with the fact he'd saved me, and nothing to do with the approval of the other gods now that I was back.

I wanted him. Because he was kind, thoughtful, and brave. Not to mention determined.

For what felt like the first time in my life, I felt settled. Like I had somewhere to belong. It wasn't perfect, but life wasn't supposed to be. Now that I was free, I was going to make the most of it. Luckily for me, having Heka by my side was a good place to start.

CHAPTER 14

I hadn't been this nervous in a while, but I wasn't sure what to expect when it came to facing Ma'at and I didn't want to say the wrong thing.

"Your Eminence," a priestess said, bowing her head to me. "If you'll follow me."

I tried to smile but feared that it came across as more of a grimace.

The priestess didn't seem to mind and led me into the audience chambers and through a row of neat indoor pools covered by beautiful trellises. It wasn't too different from what my temple would look like when it had been restored to its former glory. Hopefully my meeting with my priestesses would go well and that would happen sooner rather than later. I had no problem sharing Heka's temple with him, but my return to Karnak wouldn't feel complete until I had my own temple set up again.

"Here you are, Your Eminence," the priestess said, lifting a curtain out of the way so I can step through.

"Thank you." I ducked underneath it and entered the enclosed pool area.

Ma'at sat demurely on a bench by the side of a clear blue pool filled with a dozen fish. She scattered some food in the water for them and watched as they nibbled it all up.

"Good morning, Nephthys," she said.

"Morning."

"Why don't you take a seat?" She gestured to her left.

I took my cue from her and seated myself, folding my hands in my lap and resisting the urge to fidget.

"How are you settling back in?" Ma'at asked.

"Well, I think. I have a meeting with some of my priestesses tomorrow."

"Good. If there's anything you need, then just ask. I'll instruct my High Priestess to ensure she gives yours as much support as she needs," Ma'at said.

"You really don't have to."

"I know, I want to," she assured me. "The world has changed, but that doesn't mean that we have to turn on one another. Working together is going to be the key to our survival."

"We're already doing better than many of the other pantheons," I pointed out.

"Hmm. True. Very few of the other gods still exist from what I've heard, though perhaps they're simply laying low in places like this." She waved her hand around to indicate Karnak.

"Maybe." But I doubted it. While Seth had tried to cause a lot of problems for the rest of the gods, there hadn't been an all out war. The same couldn't be said for some of the other pantheons.

"Now, why don't you tell me everything you can about Seth's compound. We have some maps already, but maybe you could look over them for us?"

I nodded. "Can you send them to Heka's temple so I can study them in more detail?"

"Of course. I've already had copies made so you can make notes on them."

That was good. I wanted to give her as much information as I could, and I felt like I could do a better job if I had all the information laid out in front of me.

"I think one of the most important things we want to know is which gods are at the compound," Ma'at said.

I wasn't surprised. Which god was siding with who had always been one of the most interesting topics of conversation.

"I don't think there'll be any surprises. Dedun, Khnum, and Anat are all there. Though I'm not sure the latter is there by choice."

"Interesting. I'd have thought she'd have been all for Seth's domination."

"I imagine she's fed up of being treated as nothing more than a concubine when she's a trained soldier. By treating her like she's less than she is, I think he's alienated her."

"That's good information, thank you," she said.

"There are rumours about Mafdet being part of Seth's inner circle too, but I've never seen her anywhere near the compound."

Ma'at sighed and nodded. "Mafdet is a complicated one."

I frowned, trying to make sense of her statement to see if there was anything in it. "Have you heard anything about Wadjet?"

"Not really. I've heard whispers that she's Seth's prisoner, but I don't know anything about where she's been kept or if she's really there."

"Ah, that's a shame."

"You don't seem surprised?"

"I'm not," Ma'at admitted. "I've had the same reports from spies in the compound. I'd hoped you'd know more, but from Heka's report, it sounded like you didn't have much say in the day-to-day running of the compound."

"Never mind much, I didn't have any. I don't think Seth trusted me at all."

"That's a pity information wise, but at least it's made getting you here easier."

"I suppose that's one way of looking at it."

"You should know that Seth has already started sending threats about you," Ma'at said.

I frowned. "I haven't received any."

She grimaced. "He's not been addressing them to you. He's angry at the rest of us for taking you away from him."

Weirdly, her words almost hurt. By leaving the compound, I'd changed nothing. Seth didn't care that I was gone beyond that it made him look bad. This had nothing to do with me and everything to do with his ego. After thousands of years, an irrational part of me had hoped I meant more to him than that, even though I knew that wasn't true. I supposed it made it easier to push aside the guilt of leaving.

"Is there anything I can do about it?"

Ma'at shook her head. "Nothing more than you're already doing. The information you're giving us will help us find a way to stop the threats before Seth does something he regrets."

I nodded. That made sense. "So what's next?"

"What do you know about Amun? Do you know where he is?"

I paused, not wanting to say anything that went against my promise to the god, but also being aware that I couldn't lie to Ma'at without her being able to sense it.

"It's okay, I know he's there, but no one knows that I know and I want to keep it that way."

I frowned. "Why?"

"Because I have a plan for him. One that involves someone he's going to find it impossible to say no to. From what I've heard, it sounds like he's fed up with the way things are and wants them to change."

"How does that help?" A small part of me questioned why I was asking. Did I care what the situation with Amun was? He'd been friendlier than most of the gods in Seth's compound, but that didn't necessarily mean anything.

"It means that he just needs a helping hand to see the truth of the situation. I can't force him to do anything, and nor do I want to, but I'm certain he'll find his way back to us when the time is right." The satisfied smile on Ma'at's face revealed just how much she believed that.

"I hope he'll get it."

She nodded. "He will. It'll be one less god Seth has the power to draw from. And from what you're saying, it sounds like he doesn't have much to begin with."

"I don't know for sure," I hedged quickly. "I'm sure he has more allies that I don't know about."

"I'm sure he does, and there are probably some of them here at Karnak still. But I like to solve one problem at a time. And right now, I think that problem is that I've stolen too much of your time from Heka."

I chuckled. "I'm sure he doesn't mind."

"Do you?"

"Not really. I know we'll be able to spend time together later."

"Why don't you start that time now?" Ma'at suggested. "I can send you a message if I have any other questions, and you can send me one if you think of anything you've forgotten."

"Thank you." I had to admit that talking to her had been a lot easier than I'd expected it to be. Everyone talked about Ma'at as if she was a terrifying goddess that everyone had to obey at all costs, but she just seemed like a woman to me, albeit a powerful one.

I got to my feet and dipped my head in acknowledgement of her.

"Thank you, Nephthys, your information is very useful."

"You're welcome."

I left her presence feeling lighter than I had in years.

EPILOGUE

T he call to the Hall of Judgement echoed within me far louder than I'd felt it in years. For a moment, I completely forgot where I was and pushed it to the side. Seth never let me respond to the call, even if it was technically my job to make sure I did.

Except that I wasn't in Seth's compound any longer. I was at Karnak.

The Hall of Judgement was beneath me and I'd be able to take my seat amongst the judges for the first time in longer than I cared to think about.

I sat bolt upright, waking Heka in the process.

"Nephthys? Is everything all right?" he asked sleepily.

I nodded before realising that he probably couldn't see me. "Yes."

I threw off the linen sheet covering me and spun around to put my feet on the floor. I considered ringing for an attendant, but I didn't want to wake them given the late hour. Despite the intrusion to my sleep, I found the excitement growing within me.

"Are you going to explain or am I just going to have to get used to this?" he asked, clicking his fingers to turn the lamp on. There were some advantages to him being the god of magic.

"Sorry, I just got a bit excited."

"Evidently."

"I got the call to the Hall of Judgement," I explained.

"Don't you always get that?"

"Mmhmm, but I haven't been able to go for years. I wanted to, but Seth never let me."

"Ah, I see."

"And now I do. Will you tie my dress for me?" I scooted closer to the bed so he could close the ties on the back.

His fingers brushed against my skin in the most delightful way as he helped.

"I'm glad you get to go," he said.

I turned and put my arms around his neck. "Me too. Though I'm sorry I have to leave you."

"Mmm, I'm sorry about that too," he agreed. "But I'll be waiting for you when you get back."

"I'm counting on it." I leaned in and kissed him swiftly. "Sleep well."

I headed towards the door, content in the knowledge that I was going to do my duty and enter the Hall of Judgement as one of the judges. I had a purpose and a life of my own. While I was trapped in Seth's compound, I was never able to imagine either of them, but Heka's arrival in the oasis had changed all of that. The fact that I'd fallen for him only added to my happiness.

I turned to wave goodbye to him with a heart that was both light and full at the same time. I'd be back in a few hours and then I'd make sure to tell him about all the thoughts racing through my head.

And I knew he'd welcome them, just like he welcomed all the different parts of me.

The temple corridors were much quieter than during the day, which was to be expected. Hundreds of gods lived at Karnak, but only a few of us were needed in the Hall of Judgement. Only the others like me would have heard the call, everyone else would be asleep or doing whatever it was they normally did at this time.

At first, I worried about whether or not I'd be able to find my way. It had been so long since I'd made this journey, and never from Heka's temple. But I trusted my instincts and soon found myself outside the door which would lead to the hall.

I took a shaky breath. I knew that some of the gods had come to accept my presence here again, but I was sure others wouldn't be happy with me walking into a place as sacred as the Hall of Judgement.

"I know what you're thinking."

I turned to face Isis. The compassion in her eyes made it clear she'd actually guessed correctly.

"It will be okay," she promised. "All you have to do is walk in there and take your seat."

I nodded. "I know. It's just been so long..."

"You're not the only one who avoided their duty," she assured me. "We all have at one point or another."

I raised an eyebrow. "You ignored your duty?" I found that hard to believe.

"Do you not remember after Osiris..." She trailed off and glanced away.

I reached out to place a comforting hand on her arm. "Mourning him and finding him were both in service to Egypt."

She laughed softly. "But they were more in service to my grief."

"I'll give you that one. You were a mess," I admitted. "But no one would have expected you to do everything right after Osiris had passed over to the Underworld. And you came right back once you'd found a way to revive him."

"Technically, you and Heka found a way," she pointed out.

"Mostly Heka, all I did was ask." It was surprising that Seth had never put a stop to my friendship with Heka back then, but he'd probably been too preoccupied with his attempts to kill Osiris. "But if you hadn't found all the pieces of

Osiris, that wouldn't have been possible. You didn't avoid your duty then. You did your best in an awful situation."

She nodded. "How did this turn into you comforting me?" she asked with a hint of bemusement.

"I'm honestly not sure. But it did make me feel better."

"I'm glad about that. Are you ready?"

"As I'll ever be. I can't ignore the hall forever."

"Not when there's someone waiting to be judged, no."

I focused back on the door, reassured that I'd be able to enter with my sister by my side. Her support meant a lot to me, but it would mean even more to the people inside.

I pushed it open and stepped through, coming out into the elaborate hall. Everything was exactly the way I remembered it being. The forty-two judges were still arriving, and the gods who were already here talked among themselves. To my surprise, Ammit was talking with Ma'at. I hadn't expected to see her in her human form. A lot of people never even realised she had one and thought she spent all of her time asin her demon one.

A gong sounded, signalling that we should all take our seats.

Isis waved to Osiris. He smiled back at her with adoration in his eyes. Thousands of years together had done nothing to change the way they felt about one another.

"Come on." She tugged me towards our seats.

It was strange to think that no one else was aware of the enormity of this moment for me, but as I took my seat, it felt as if everything had fallen into place. This was where I was supposed to be, doing what I was supposed to do.

Ammit was in her demon form once more, with her powerful crocodile jaws poised in case the soul's heart would need devouring. Osiris sat on his throne, while Anubis waited next to the huge golden scales with Ma'at by his side, her feather perched in her hands.

The double doors swung open, and the familiar sight of a soul making their way through to be judged made it really sink in for me.

I was finally back where I belonged.

***

Thank you for reading *Empress Of The Dark*, I hope you enjoyed it. If you want to continue the *Forgotten Gods* series, you can with Wadjet's story, *Serpent Of The Crown*: http://books2read.com/serpentofthecrown

You can also download a *Forgotten Gods* story, *Priestess Of Truth*, to join my newsletter and stay up to date with future releases: https://books.authorlauragreenwood.co.uk/iqknd8er35

AUTHOR NOTE

Thank you for reading *Empress Of The Dark*, I hope you enjoyed it.

If you want to read the Forgotten Gods Universe in the order of events, then you should go to the complete *Queen Of Gods* trilogy (Hathor and Amun's story) before *Serpent Of The Crown*. If you're joining the series after reading the previous books, then you might already know that Rhodopis' story was book three, *Servant Of Chaos*. You can also find Isis and Nut's stories as part of the *Forgotten Gods: Origins* series in *Queen Of The Two Lands* and *Mistress Of Sky And Stars* respectively. The origins series is set in ancient times and deals with some of the creation myths of the New Kingdom.

The game Nephthys and Heka play, Hounds and Jackals, is a real Ancient Egyptian board game. The rules they were playing by is one interpretation of the board and pieces found in various tombs. Upon researching the game, I found it reminded me of games like Ludo or Boggle, though I also found some people saying it reminded them of Snakes and Ladders. Normally when my characters in the Forgotten Gods universe play a game on page, it's Senet, but I decided that it was time to introduce another one!

I would also like to add a note that while he is the antagonist of the Forgotten Gods universe, Seth is not inherently an evil force in mythology. There are several creation myths that suggest he is - such as the one where he cuts Osiris into pieces and usurps him, and then fights Horus, and that's the history the characters have in the Forgotten Gods Universe. However, most of those creation stories hail from the New Kingdom of Ancient Egypt - thousands of years after Seth came into being. I've tried to acknowledge this in the way some of the characters accept that Seth needs to continue being because chaos is important to the world, even while he is clearly being an antagonist. I do have some ideas about representing the other side of Seth in a different universe (I don't feel like I can do it in the Forgotten Gods Universe due to the things he's done on page), so make sure you're part of my <u>Facebook Reader Group</u> or <u>mailing list</u>. for news about that.

The marriages between the gods have been done in the same way that they would have been during parts of Egyptian history. When a couple moved in together, they were determined to be married, and there would often be a family celebration to go along with it. If the couple wanted to get divorced, then one of them would move out of their house and that would be the end of their marriage.

And finally, a quick note on genetics in the Forgotten Gods Universe. Upon researching, I discovered that a lot of the gods and goddesses of the Egyptian pantheon were put into family groups based on what kind of forces they were the gods/goddesses of, rather than anything like genetics. For that reason, none of the gods are related by blood - which also serves to erase some of the incestuous matches (that were also made because of forces that went well together and not necessarily anything to do with the stories themselves). Some of the gods/goddesses do continue to feel family bonds to others, but that is through personal choice on each character's part.

Stay safe & happy reading!

- Laura

ALSO BY LAURA GREENWOOD

Signed Paperback & Merchandise:

You can find signed paperbacks, hardcovers, and merchandise based on my series (including stickers, magnets, face masks, and more!) via my website:

https://www.authorlauragreenwood.co.uk/p/shop.html

Series List:

* denotes a completed series

The Obscure World

- Ashryn Barker*

- Grimalkin Academy: Kittens*

- Grimalkin Academy: Catacombs*

- <u>City Of Blood</u>*

- <u>Grimalkin Academy: Stakes</u>*

- <u>Supernatural Retrieval Agency</u>*

- <u>The Black Fan</u>

- <u>Sabre Woods Academy</u>*

- <u>Scythe Grove Academy</u>*

- <u>The Shifter Season</u>

- <u>Cauldron Coffee Shop</u>

- <u>Obscure Academy</u>

- <u>Stonerest Academy</u>

- <u>Obscure World: Holidays</u>

The Forgotten Gods World

- <u>The Queen of Gods</u>*

- <u>Forgotten Gods</u>

- <u>Forgotten Gods: Origins</u>

The Grimm World

- <u>Grimm Academy</u>*

- <u>Fate Of The Crown</u>*

- <u>Once Upon An Academy Series</u>

- <u>The Princess Competition</u>

The Paranormal Council Universe

- <u>The Paranormal Council Series</u>

- <u>The Fae Queen Of Winter Trilogy</u>*

- <u>Paranormal Criminal Investigations</u>

- <u>MatchMater Paranormal Dating App</u>*

- <u>The Necromancer Council</u>*

- <u>Return Of The Fae</u>*

Other Series

- <u>The Apprentice Of Anubis</u>

- <u>Beyond The Curse</u>

- <u>Untold Tales</u>*

- <u>The Dragon Duels</u>*

- <u>Rosewood Academy</u>

- <u>ME</u>*

- <u>Seven Wardens</u>*, co-written with Skye MacKinnon

- <u>Tales Of Clan Robbins</u>, co-written with L.A. Boruff

- <u>Firehouse Witches</u>*, co-written with Lacey Carter Andersen & L.A. Boruff

- <u>Purple Oasis</u>, co-created series with Arizona Tape

Twin Souls Universe, all series co-written with Arizona Tape

- <u>Twin Souls</u>*

- <u>Dragon Soul</u>*

- <u>The Renegade Dragons</u>*

- <u>The Vampire Detective</u>*

- <u>Amethyst's Wand Shop Mysteries</u>

- <u>The Necromancer Morgue Mysteries</u>

Mountain Shifters Universe, all series co-written with L.A. Boruff

About the Author

- Valentine Pride*

- Magic and Metaphysics Academy*

Laura is a USA Today Bestselling Author of paranormal, fantasy, urban fantasy, and contemporary romance. When she's not writing, she drinks a lot of tea, tries to resist French macarons, and works towards a diploma in Egyptology. She lives in the UK, where most of her books are set. Laura specialises in quick reads, whether you're looking for a swoonworthy romance for the bath, or an action-packed adventure for your latest journey, you'll find the perfect match amongst her books!

Follow the Author

- Website: www.authorlauragreenwood.co.uk

- Mailing List: www.authorlauragreenwood.co.uk/p/mailing-list-sign-up.html

- Facebook Group: http://facebook.com/groups/theparanormalcouncil

- Facebook Page: http://facebook.com/authorlauragreenwood

- Bookbub: www.bookbub.com/authors/laura-greenwood

www.ingramcontent.com/pod-product-compliance
Lightning Source LLC
Chambersburg PA
CBHW020959160726
47994CB00006B/2305